D0875671

TIME TWISTERS

TIME UNDER THE SEA

Calico

An Imprint of Magic Wagon
abdopublishing.com

BY KATHRYN LAY   ILLUSTRATED BY DAVE BARDIN

TO MOM, FOR BELIEVING IN AND ENCOURAGING MY WRITING FROM THE BEGINNING. —KL

FOR MY MOM, WHO GAVE ME MY FIRST SKETCHBOOK AND HAS NEVER STOPPED GIVING. —DB

abdopublishing.com

Published by Magic Wagon, a division of ABDO, PO Box 398166, Minneapolis, Minnesota 55439. Copyright © 2017 by Abdo Consulting Group, Inc. International copyrights reserved in all countries. No part of this book may be reproduced in any form without written permission from the publisher. Calico™ is a trademark and logo of Magic Wagon.

Printed in the United States of America, North Mankato, Minnesota.
102016
012017

Written by Kathryn Lay
Illustrated by Dave Bardin
Edited by Megan M. Gunderson
Designed by Laura Mitchell

Publisher's Cataloging-in-Publication Data

Names: Lay, Kathryn, author. | Bardin, Dave, illustrator.
Title: Time under the sea / by Kathryn Lay ; illustrated by Dave Bardin.
Description: Minneapolis, MN : Magic Wagon, 2017. | Series: Time twisters;
    Book 4
Summary: Luis, Tyler, Casey, and robot cat Steel travel to an underwater
    future using Tesla's Time Twister, where they face sea monsters and
    hope to finally get Uncle Cyrus unstuck in time.
Identifiers: LCCN 2016947667 | ISBN 9781624021800 (lib. bdg.) |
    ISBN 978162402401 (ebook) | ISBN 9781624022708 (Read-to-me ebook)
Subjects: LCSH: Time travel--Juvenile fiction. | Best friends--Juvenile fiction.
    Adventure and adventurers--Juvenile fiction. | Survival--Juvenile
    fiction.
Classification: DDC [Fic]--dc23
LC record available at http://lccn.loc.gov/2016947667

TABLE

OF

CONTENTS

READY?

Luis sat in the lawn chair on his back porch. He stared at the shed at the end of his yard.

Just like every morning for the last two days, he waited for his best friends Tyler and Casey Jenson. His father complained that they spent too much time hanging around the house instead of doing more interesting things at the end of spring break. If only he knew!

Luis thought several times about telling him about the three times they had gone forward and back in time. But he felt sure his dad would stop them from going again. And they had to try once more to help his great-great-great-great-uncle Cyrus get back to his own time.

MEEOWWWW! SPPPPTTT!

Luis jumped up when Tyler's robot cat, Steel, rolled across his foot.

Tyler sat down in the chair next to Luis and Casey flopped onto the porch. Her magician-style jacket full of tools and gadgets rattled.

"Still no luck with getting Steel's meow to sound normal, huh?" Luis asked.

Tyler set his forearm crutches on the ground. "Nope. I think that cat is messing with my head."

Luis grinned. He hated to admit that he liked the weird cat. Steel had helped them when they were fighting aliens in space, ghosts and crooks in a haunted house, and flaming scarabs in an Egyptian pyramid.

"Have you heard anything from Uncle Cyrus?" Casey asked. She pulled a metal box of small gears and wheels and a screwdriver from her pockets.

Luis watched Casey take apart the gadget, then put it back together again.

"How can I hear from Uncle Cyrus when you have Steel with the two of you?" Luis said. "I think I need to keep it here since it needs to be near Tesla's Time Twister for Uncle Cyrus to talk through it."

Tyler nodded. "Yeah, I agree. If we don't hear something soon, we'll be going back to school."

"And our dad is afraid we're bored, so he's talking about taking us to a cabin that a friend of his owns," Casey said. "We can't leave now. You can't Time Twist alone."

"My dad's been trying to get me to go somewhere away from the house, too. I told him the three of us might go to the movies today, in case he comes home and we're not here," Luis said.

"You mean, like not here or anywhere in this time?" Casey said. "If we don't go soon, Cyrus may really be stuck in the machine's pull on time forever. That would be awful."

Luis opened his mouth to agree when Steel began to shake. His tail twisted in a circle and his eyes glowed red.

Luis grabbed the robot. "Is that you, Uncle Cyrus?"

Steel's voice box crackled. "Yes, Luis. But you must hurry to the machine. I have been sent to another event in time, and I need your help."

Luis and his friends jumped up.

"Okay, this is it. Maybe if we solve this adventure and find another item from Tesla, Uncle Cyrus can finally go home."

Casey grabbed Steel and took off fast.

Tyler moved quickly across the grass. He could run a lot faster than people gave him credit for. Especially when the fifth-grade bully Greg Dover was chasing him. Or an Egyptian crocodile-lion-hippo goddess.

Luis ran to the shed and pulled the strange tree-shaped key from his pocket. He fit it into the large lock, turned it, and stepped back as sparks shot out and the lock fell to the ground.

"Hurry!" he shouted to his friends.

Casey ran into the shed and held the door open for her brother. She shut it behind him.

They walked across the large shed to the tarp-covered machine on its wooden platform. Luis and Casey yanked off the tarp.

Luis set the combination lock on the machine to 10, 10, 10. Their fathers had used their ages to set it. Luis wondered if his dad hadn't been thinking hard enough, or thought it would be too obvious for Luis and his friends to guess.

The door of Tesla's Time Twister slid open and they went inside.

They quickly found their seats. Luis put his hands on the spot where he had to set the dates on the machine.

"Okay Uncle Cyrus, where are you?" Luis asked. "What date do we set?"

Steel bumped into the control panel, then backed up and rolled forward until it bumped the panel again with its nose.

"The date to set is March 20, 2175," Cyrus's voice said.

"All right, into the future," Tyler said. "Maybe robots will do all our work for us."

Luis shook his head. "I hope not. How many science fiction movies are there about robots who take over humans? Lots!"

He leaned over and set the dials to March, 20, 2175. He smiled at his friends. What kind of problem would they have to solve this time? He hoped it wasn't more aliens.

"Ready?" he asked.

"Ready!" Casey said.

"Oh yeah," Tyler added.

Luis pulled the lever next to the dates. The room began to spin. He knew it wasn't the machine moving. Somehow, they traveled through time because of the machine, but Tesla's Time Twister did not go with them.

Luis kept his eyes open this time. He watched his friends' bodies twist through time. Like before, he felt like they were in a whirling tornado. Mist surrounded him and he could not see the Time Twister any more. This time, the whirling tornado around him looked like water.

A water cyclone, Luis thought.

Strange shadows seemed to swim around him. His ears popped like they did when he dived off the high dive into the deep end of the pool at the recreation center. He opened and closed his mouth until the popping feeling stopped.

The feeling of movement stopped. Luis heard the sound of breaking waves. He opened his eyes.

Luis stood on the deck of some kind of boat. All around was water. The waves beat against the boat.

Dark clouds above him rumbled with thunder. Lightning flashed in the clouds. Wind whipped across the deck of the ship, blowing an odd-looking flag back and forth.

Luis rubbed his eyes as salty water sprayed his face. The flag showed a city under a glass dome. Fish swam around the city and a large letter A was stitched onto the flag.

"Where are we?" Tyler asked. He sat on the deck next to Steel. "I don't think this salty air is good for my cat."

Casey pulled her coat tight. "It's not good for any of us. I'm cold."

Luis looked around the deck of the boat. He realized it wasn't just a boat. It was a huge ship. It shone of black metal. There were no masts or oars.

Luis walked across the deck, surprised that the metal wasn't slippery with the waves crashing up over the sides.

"Hey, you three! What are you doing up here? Get below immediately!" a voice shouted.

Luis and his friends turned. A tall man in a dark blue suit walked toward them. He glared at them as he held his hat on his head to keep it blowing off in the wind.

Tyler let go of one of his crutches and whipped his hand to his forehead in a salute.

"What's going on?" Luis whispered.

"It's an admiral," Tyler whispered back. "And I don't think we are officers this time."

Luis and Casey saluted.

The tall man saluted back. "I asked you three why you are here. Didn't you hear the horn blast? We are diving in a few moments. Look, the flag is dropping already. This storm is a fierce one. We need to return home. Haven't you been told of the distress calls?"

Luis nodded. "Yes, sir. We were going now." He looked around. "And how do we get below?"

The admiral frowned. "Don't play games with me, son. This may be your first trip on the *Neptune*, but I know you were all briefed before we left."

They all stared at one another a moment. The admiral sighed.

"Follow me," he said.

Tyler whispered to Luis. "It's a submarine!"

Someone dressed in a blue uniform passed by them. He saluted and said, "The rest of the deck is clear, Admiral Jefferson."

The admiral saluted back and kept walking.

As they walked across the deck to an open hatch above a set of stairs, Luis cleared his throat and said, "I'm sorry to ask, but where is home, sir?"

The admiral didn't turn, but Luis saw his shoulders stiffen. "Close that hatch behind you. And where else would home be for the crew of the *Neptune*? New Atlantis. We're heading back to New Atlantis, the best city in the sea. For a little while, anyway."

Casey gasped. "Atlantis? It must be beautiful."

Admiral Jefferson nodded. "Yes. And right now, the most dangerous place to live if we can't stop the giant sea creatures that are attacking the city. That's my job. And now it's your job."

They came to the bottom of the steps.

"Now, get to your stations and do your job. We are counting on you."

Horns blasted around them. Luis's ears popped again as the submarine dove beneath the ocean waves.

ABOARD THE NEPTUNE

Bells clanged all around the submarine. People in gray and blue uniforms rushed up and down the corridors. Luis had imagined a submarine being tight and narrow, but this wasn't like any submarine he'd seen in the movies.

"Wow, it's as big as a cruise ship," Casey whispered.

Luis watched the admiral shouting orders to crewmen who were working on 3-D screen computers. Screens on the sides of the large control room showed the undersea world around them.

Fish of all colors and sizes swam past them. Tall blades of seaweed waved as if blown in the wind. Larger sea creatures with bulging eyes or rows of sharp teeth paused to peer into the outside cameras.

After a few moments, the frenzy of the crew calmed. "Admiral Jefferson, are these young crew here by your invitation?" a woman in a dark gray uniform asked.

The admiral turned, looking surprised when he saw Luis and his friends.

"Why are you three still here? You should be at your duties. We'll be approaching New Atlantis in a half hour. All hands will be needed as we maneuver by whatever creatures are attacking it," Admiral Jefferson said.

He glanced at Steel. "And no pets allowed out of your quarters. Unless this is a working bot you have?"

Tyler nodded. "Uh, yes, sir. This robot is very important to our work."

"Fine," the admiral said. "But keep him from under foot. Return to your duties on C Deck. We need the research on the sea monsters uploaded by the time New Atlantis is in sight."

Luis and his friends saluted, then hurried out of the control room.

The corridor gleamed with shiny metal. The *Neptune* moved smoothly through the water.

"This is amazing," Casey said. "A futuristic submarine? An underwater city? Sea monsters?"

Steel rolled ahead of them and stopped. The robot bounced up and down and cocked its head.

"I am confused at our purpose for being here so far into the future," Uncle Cyrus said. "How could Tesla have left me anything to help me get home in this time and place?"

Luis stopped to look at a map on the wall of the submarine. It glowed red. He reached out to touch it. A blip appeared on the map.

"I think that's me," Luis said. He walked a few steps down the corridor.

Tyler said, "Yes, the red dot moves with you. Cool!"

Luis walked back and said, "We need to find C Deck and figure out why we're supposed to be there. Sounds like a library or something if we're researching these sea monsters."

Casey pressed her finger on the map. Another dot appeared.

"Where is C Deck?" she asked.

The dot began to move down the corridor.

"Follow that dot!" Luis said.

They walked along the corridor, stopping every time they saw a new map on the wall. The moving dot turned left at the next intersecting corridor.

Other crew walked past them, moving in and out of corridors and rooms. Luis bumped into a man in a gray suit as he followed the dot on the next map.

"Oops, sorry," Luis said.

The man grinned. "Sorry. I wasn't paying attention. I guess we're all a little nervous about going back home."

Casey asked, "Nervous? About going to New Atlantis? But it must be wonderful."

"Yes, it's an amazing city. People pay a lot to live there. But since the attacks, the city is looking to us for protection. So far, we've not been able to stop the creatures."

Steel rolled up.

MEOWWWW! KA-CHING!

The crewman laughed. "Your bot seems out of whack. Take it to Bot Repair when you get a chance."

Tyler grinned. "Bot Repair? Sounds like my kind of place."

Luis said, "I guess we'd better get to C Deck like the admiral told us."

The man nodded. "Yes, you must be the sea creature experts the admiral sent for to learn about these things and how to stop their attacks."

"We are?" Luis asked.

"Aren't you?" the man asked. "The library is the fourth door down. Good luck. All of New Atlantis is counting on us. And, on you three most of all."

He turned and walked away.

"Wow, sounds like we've got important work to do," Luis said. "I don't know anything about undersea creatures, except what I read about and see in the movies."

"Amazing!" Casey said as they walked into the large room. Walls were lined with bookshelves and a metal table was covered with 3-D photographs of large, strange creatures.

Luis picked up some of the photographs. The monsters seemed to jump off the page.

"Wow, they're 3-D without glasses," Casey said. She rummaged in her coat pocket and pulled out a set of plastic 3-D glasses.

She said, "I wonder how double 3-D looks." She put on the glasses and took one of the photographs from Luis's hand.

"Eeek!" she screamed, dropping it. She pulled off the glasses. "That's too much reality."

Luis put each photo on the table side by side. It looked like an ocean of fins, pointed teeth, and bulbous eyes. One creature had hands with claws. Another had a tail that looked like his mom's best steak knives, except much bigger and sharper.

Then he pulled out a photograph of the underwater city.

It was a city built on sand. Tall buildings rose several stories high. They were the color of red sandstone and seemed to shine in the water. People stood in the streets and outside of homes that reminded him of the ceramic houses in his fish tank.

Coral gardens of reds and purples brightened the areas outside the houses and buildings.

The whole city was covered by a clear bubble. It was as beautiful as Casey had said it would be.

"It's horrible!" Casey said.

Luis agreed. He knew she wasn't talking about the underwater city. Surrounding the city were the creatures they had seen in the other photographs. Each one was as big as the tallest buildings. The sea monsters' snouts were pressed against the bubble as if they were ready to break their way inside.

Luis looked closer and saw that the people standing around were looking at the creatures from inside the bubble. They were screaming.

Luis felt like screaming, too.

He looked at Steel. "Uncle Cyrus, I think we're ready to go home now. Tesla couldn't have sent us here."

Uncle Cyrus's voice seemed to shake from Steel's voice box. "If I had control of the Time Twister, I would send you home immediately. But we're all stuck here until our task is done."

Casey pointed to the 3-D pictures. "Or until we're eaten by Godzilla fish."

The smoothness of the submarine trip ended as the ship lurched to a stop.

"All hands on deck!" a voice shouted from an intercom on the desk. "The sea monsters are attacking the *Neptune.*"

Luis turned to run out of the room. Tyler grabbed his arm. "It looks like our job is to figure out some kind of way to fight these things. We'd better move fast and go through some of these books."

Luis put Steel on the table as Casey began thumbing through books on the shelf.

From somewhere outside the ship came a roar that rattled the sub.

SEA MONSTERS!

The submarine shook and books fell to the floor. Casey dropped to her knees and looked through them.

"Here's a book to look at," she said. She held it out to him.

Luis took it and read the cover. *Sea Monsters of the World and Their Habitats.*

He put it on the table and flipped through it.

"There are tons of sea monsters in here," Tyler said. "Where did they all come from?"

Luis shrugged. He stopped at a page with a nasty looking creature. It was long and had a large mouth with double rows of sharp teeth. Its scales looked like armor and were bright red.

"I saw that one in a 3-D picture," Luis said.

Casey bent over and read, "The Monolith Sea Dragon was discovered in 2165 by Dr. Sykes in a formerly unexplored cavern near New Atlantis. He witnessed the creature shooting flames and promptly associated it with the legendary land dragon. Dr. Sykes's expeditions have found other such strange creatures around this undersea cavern, believed to have been above ground before the Great Earthquake of 2055."

"Wow," Luis said. "This Dr. Sykes is one brave guy. Let's look and see if there are more creatures he found that look like the ones attacking New Atlantis."

They looked through every page of the large book and found seven creatures that were the same as the ones in the 3-D photos.

"We need to show this to the admiral. Maybe he can find this Dr. Sykes," Casey said.

"That is an excellent idea, Casey," Uncle Cyrus said. Steel's eyes glowed red. "What you need is an expert who has studied these creatures if you want to learn how to beat them."

Casey grabbed the book and Luis picked up Steel.

MEOWWWRRRP! PLLLPP!

Tyler said, "I want to take Steel to that bot shop the man told us about. I'd love to see what other robots they have on this submarine."

"Sorry Tyler, not now," Luis said. "We've got to talk to Admiral Jefferson first. Maybe later."

Tyler frowned, but then he nodded.

They went back into the corridor. Luis said, "Do we turn right or left at the next corridor?"

Casey touched one of the wall maps and said, "Control room!"

A red dot appeared and moved along the map. It turned right and they followed it. They could hear the admiral shouting as they got closer.

"We've got to outmaneuver those beasts!" Admiral Jefferson shouted. "Drop one hundred feet and we'll slip around to the back docking station."

"Sir, if one follows us, it might break into New Atlantis while we are docking," a red-haired woman said.

The admiral nodded. "You're right. Then we must stand and fight first. Prepare the lasers."

Several crew members used holographic screens, swiping their hands over them until Luis saw a picture of a long tube. It glowed orange.

A crewman punched numbers on a keypad. "Lasers 1 and 2 are ready, Admiral," he said.

Luis turned to a holographic screen showing the outside of the submarine. A huge creature loomed. It looked like a hammerhead shark with clawed flippers, and it was charging toward the ship.

An orange beam of light shot from the submarine. It went past the sea monster.

"You missed!" Admiral Jefferson shouted.

A second beam of light hit the creature in its bony skull. The sea monster spun backward and sunk downward.

The control room echoed with cheers.

"Good shot," the admiral said.

Casey pointed toward the screen. "Look again, sir!"

The sea monster was coming straight for them again. It had a burned spot on its head but otherwise seemed unharmed.

The monster rammed the ship. Sirens sounded and a voice yelled from an intercom.

"We're taking on water, sir. We need to get back to base."

Admiral Jefferson stared at the screen as the sea monster made another pass around the submarine.

"We'd better head for home before it hits us again," Admiral Jefferson said. "Go around to Dock 3 between the seaweed and do your best

to lose this creature. We're just going to have to risk it at this point."

He looked at Luis and his friends.

"Are you back? I hope you have some good news."

Tyler pointed to the book in Luis's hand.

"We haven't figured out how to get rid of these creatures, but we think we found someone who might know a lot more about them than anyone here," Tyler said.

Luis opened the book and showed several pictures and descriptions of strange-looking and giant sea monsters.

"The man who took all these photographs is someone named Dr. Sykes. If we can find him, maybe he can come to New Atlantis and tell us how to fight the sea monsters," Luis said.

The admiral took the book from Luis's hand. He flipped through it until he found a photograph of a man.

"This is Dr. Sykes," Admiral Jefferson said. "He's one of the most knowledgeable marine biologists in the world."

Casey grinned. "Great! Then can you call him when we get to New Atlantis or something?"

The room was silent. The crew worked quietly to dock the submarine at New Atlantis. Some glanced at the admiral and shifted as if they were uncomfortable.

Admiral Jefferson held the book out to Luis.

"I don't have to call him, young man. I know exactly where Dr. Sykes is now."

Luis waited. He had a bad feeling there was something wrong.

Admiral Jefferson sighed and said, "He's already at New Atlantis. He's been in a coma since his last expedition to the cave discussed in this book."

"A coma?" Luis asked. "Was he hurt by the sea monsters?"

Admiral Jefferson motioned for them to follow him. He led them down the corridor and up a set of metal steps to a paneled room.

"My quarters," he said.

They walked inside and all sat on a large leather sofa.

Luis had thought that the captain's quarters on the spaceship were amazing. But the admiral's quarters were even better. Windows surrounded the room. Small, colorful fish swam past them like in a fancy fish tank. The water glowed from the lights off of the submarine.

"I didn't want to talk about Dr. Sykes's condition in front of the others," the admiral said.

Luis leaned forward. Steel rolled across the floor and stopped beside the admiral's foot. Luis hoped that Uncle Cyrus wouldn't start speaking.

"When Dr. Sykes returned from his last trip, he was found inside his submarine, blubbering like a lost child. His crew was missing. No one could get him to answer questions about what happened," Admiral Jefferson said.

"That's scary," Casey said.

The admiral sat behind his desk and stared out the window beside him. "Dr. Sykes is an old friend. He's been on the *Neptune* many times and my crew knows him well. I had never seen him act so strangely. He stared at the walls of his hospital room and spoke four words over and over. Then, he fell into a coma."

Luis and his friends leaned closer to the admiral.

"What did he say?" Tyler asked.

Admiral Jefferson looked him in the eyes and said, "New Atlantis is doomed."

New Atlantis

Luis leaned back on the soft leather couch in the admiral's comfortable quarters. He watched the colorful fish swim by the glass windows that lined the room. He could hear quiet music coming from a speaker in a corner of the room.

It was beautiful, but all around them was danger. They were on a submarine headed to an underwater city that was doomed. And the only man who might know something about the sea monsters attacking the city was in a coma.

"Admiral, we are preparing to dock into New Atlantis through the hidden path," a voice said over the loudspeaker. "Radar shows that the city is surrounded by at least half a dozen of the giant creatures."

Admiral Jefferson stood. "I'm on my way."

He turned to the kids. "Once we leave the *Neptune,* I will take you to the hospital to see Dr. Sykes. Perhaps you can be there to question him when . . . if he wakes. Do any of you have engineering and computer operating abilities?"

Tyler raised his hand. "I do, sir. I built my robot cat. And I hope to go into space one day."

The admiral laughed. "We conquered space long ago. You should be on one of the space stations or space ports instead of underwater."

"I would love that!" Tyler said. He rubbed his hands together.

Luis knew his friend was enjoying all the possibilities in this time, with his interest in robotics and computers, but he needed Tyler and Casey to help him find a way to stop the sea monsters from destroying New Atlantis. And they needed to figure out where Tesla could have left them a clue in the future.

Admiral Jefferson told them how to get to the door that would lead them off the submarine once they were docked.

"Wait for me to take you to the hospital. There will be panic in the streets, and it will be safer if you stay with me," Admiral Jefferson said.

Luis followed the admiral's instructions. The room by the exit door was crowded with people waiting to get off the *Neptune*.

"Did you hear? They say on the north side of the city, there is a crack in the dome," a woman said.

A man behind her waved his arms. "It's a death trap here. We've got to find a way to evacuate everyone."

The people murmured in fear.

A heavyset man cleared his throat. "It would take days to get enough transports down here to evacuate New Atlantis. And besides, those creatures could destroy any other submarines trying to get inside the city."

Luis could feel a panic starting in the room. If the crew of this submarine were this afraid, the people in the underwater city must be terrified.

"There's nowhere for them to go," Casey whispered. "They're just trapped underwater."

Tyler said, "Don't forget. We're trapped here, too. At least until we find what Tesla left."

Casey squeezed Steel. "We can't stay here, Cyrus. We have to get back home."

Cyrus's voice was strained. "I'm sorry, Casey. I agree with you, but I cannot control the Time Twister."

A light above them flashed green and a large door lowered.

The crowd moved forward onto a wooden platform.

Luis squinted. "Wow, it's brighter down here than I expected."

A woman gave Luis a wide-eyed stare. "Young man, everyone knows that the lights in New Atlantis run by water power."

Casey giggled, "I guess she told you. We're going to have to be careful how uninformed we sound. Apparently New Atlantis is well-known around the world."

They followed the crowd to the edge of the platform. Stairs led down to streets. Some people walked, but others rode on metal chairs that sped over the roads like small floating cars.

"We can wait here for the admiral," Luis said.

They leaned against a railing and looked at the strange city. It was full of glittering buildings and red and purple grass. Trees that looked like coral stood tall along every street.

"It looks a little like a regular city," Tyler said.

"Except for that," Casey said, pointing to the glass dome covering the city.

"And that!" Luis shouted.

Two of the huge sea monsters swam past the city. They slowed and peered inside. They were as big as the buildings.

People screamed and hurried through the streets and into buildings.

Admiral Jefferson walked out of the *Neptune* and started down the steps to the street below. "Come with me. Quickly."

Luis and his friends followed the admiral through the now quiet streets. Abandoned chair-cars lay on the roads and sidewalks. Luis could see wide-eyed faces looking through windows.

Suddenly, the street moved below their feet.

"Earthquake!" Tyler yelled.

Steel wobbled on the road and tipped over.

Luis picked up the robot. He stood up in time to see one of the sea creatures slam into the dome over the city.

"That's the strongest glass ever made," Admiral Jefferson said. "But it may not hold."

"Is there a way to get all of these people out?" Casey asked.

The admiral turned right at a stoplight and then walked into a tall building. The sign over the door said: New Atlantis Memorial Hospital.

"We've sent for help," Admiral Jefferson said, "but it may not arrive in time. We've been commissioned by world leaders to do our best to remove or destroy the threat."

Tyler shook his head. "It would be too bad to destroy such unusual creatures."

They followed the admiral up a flight of stairs, down a hall, and into a room.

Soft lights lit the room. There was a bed in the center, a rolling table, and one chair. Panels on the wall beeped quietly, lit up with symbols and arrows. Tubes ran from the wall to the arm of the man lying in the bed.

Admiral Jefferson stood beside the bed. "This is Dr. Sykes. He has no physical injuries. It is only his mind. Doctors believe he may even be able to hear us. It is the trauma of what he has seen that has put him in this condition."

Luis looked down at the man in the bed. He expected someone old. Someone who had been at sea for more years than their fathers' ages put together.

Instead, the man lying in the bed looked to be the same age as Luis's father. Luis thought the man might be around thirty-five. Yet, he was already an expert on sea creatures and discoveries under the deepest part of the oceans.

"Sykes?" The admiral leaned closer to his friend. "I have brought you visitors. They want to help us find a way to stop the creatures that are attacking the city."

Dr. Sykes didn't move.

"He doesn't say anything?" Casey asked.

Admiral Jefferson shook his head. "Not since those final words of warning. He hasn't moved a finger, twitched an eyelid, or wrinkled his nose. It's a mystery."

Luis moved closer to the bed. "Hello, sir. My friends and I really want to help New Atlantis. But we sure could use your help. You seem to be the only one who really knows anything about the creatures."

Dr. Sykes lay still.

The admiral moved toward the door. "I must talk with the city council about ideas for distracting these creatures. I'll leave you three here. Talk with Dr. Sykes. If he can hear you as the doctors think, maybe you can get through to him."

He walked out the door, pulling it closed behind him.

Tyler leaned forward, steadying a crutch against the bed. "Hello in there!" he shouted at Dr. Sykes's ear.

"Stop that," Casey said.

She pulled a metal box from one of her pockets and began taking it apart. Whenever she was thinking, she liked to work with her gadgets.

Luis walked to the window in the room. He looked down and saw that people had returned to the streets. A little boy looked up at him and waved from the side chair of his mother's chair-car. Luis waved back.

"So what do we do now?" Tyler asked.

Steel rolled closer to the bed and then under it. From there, Uncle Cyrus's voice said, "I suggest you try talking with him as you were instructed."

Luis turned back to the bed. "Hi there. I don't know if you can hear us, but we've traveled through time from your past. We need to find something and it looks like we need to help stop New Atlantis from being destroyed."

Casey gasped and pointed. "I think his eyes twitched."

Luis watched Dr. Sykes's face. Nothing.

"So, we were hoping you could help us," Luis continued. "We found your book and we've heard that you were in a cave with some of these sea monsters. If you'd just wake up, you could help save the city and help us get back home. We came here through a time machine. Tesla's Time Twister."

Dr. Sykes's eyes popped open. He sat up in bed like a spring had pushed him forward.

Casey screamed and Tyler yelped.

Luis jumped back.

Dr. Sykes looked right at Luis and said, "Time travelers! I've been waiting for you. Let's get to work!"

Delicious Orange Goo

Dr. Sykes pushed the call button over and over again.

"Uh, shouldn't you lie back and calm down?" Luis asked.

Dr. Sykes just laughed. "I've been lying down for too long."

He pressed on the button again.

A nurse ran into the room. Her face was red.

"Stop pressing the button! I'm here now," she said. "What is so urgent?

Her eyes went wide. Her mouth fell open. She dropped the chart in her hands.

"Dr. Sykes?" she gasped.

Moments later, she was yelling down the hall. Two more nurses and a doctor came into the room. When they saw Dr. Sykes sitting up and petting Steel, they stopped as if they'd run into a wall.

Casey put her hand over her mouth and giggled.

Dr. Sykes pointed to the IV in his arm and the wires attached to his chest. "Get these things off of me. We have work to do to save New Atlantis!"

The doctor rushed to the bed and looked into Dr. Sykes's eyes. He listened to his chest, felt his pulse, and peered into his mouth.

"Stop that," Dr. Sykes said. "Let me out of this bed right now."

"But," the doctor sputtered, "you must rest after . . . we need to run some tests and . . ."

Dr. Sykes shook his finger at the doctor. "You need to get these things off of me now and bring me my clothes. Or do you want those creatures outside coming inside the dome?"

The doctor looked at Luis, Tyler, and Casey. He looked back at Dr. Sykes. He sighed and turned to the nurses. "Dr. Sykes is to be discharged immediately."

The doctor walked out of the room, shaking his head and muttering.

Luis and his friends were hurried out of the room while the nurses unhooked and helped dress Dr. Sykes.

"Wow, that was wild," Tyler said. "We need to find the admiral and tell him Dr. Sykes is okay now!"

Luis leaned against a wall. "But did you hear what he said when he woke up? He knows we're time travelers and he's been waiting for us."

Steel's ears twisted. "It is possible that he found something that belonged to my friend, Nikola Tesla. Perhaps Tesla left something here in the future with instructions in case I was still trapped in time."

The door next to them opened and Dr. Sykes walked out. He wore a silver jumpsuit and thick glasses. Luis thought he looked like someone from a steampunk play his dad took him to once.

"Well, don't dawdle," Dr. Sykes said. "Let's find Admiral Jefferson and get the crew gathered together on the *Neptune*. We have a lot to talk about and a vital journey to make."

Luis cleared his throat as they walked down the hallway to the stairs. "Sir, you said you'd been waiting for us. What did you mean? And why do you believe me when I say we are time travelers?"

Dr. Sykes slapped Luis on the back. "Of course I believe you. I can't wait to talk with you three more. But for now, I'll quickly tell you that there is something in the sea monsters' cavern that you have to see."

"A message?" Casey asked.

"From Nikola Tesla?" Tyler added.

Sykes stopped. "Yes. I feel it must mean something to you three. The answer to getting the sea monsters to leave New Atlantis alone may also be found in that cave."

They walked downstairs and onto the street. Luis dodged the people and chair-cars as he and his friends ran behind Dr. Sykes. Luis looked above him and could see the huge creatures swimming back and forth.

"Shouldn't there be other fish all around us?" Casey asked.

Dr. Sykes nodded. "It is normally a beautiful and colorful place beyond the dome. People sit in the parks and watch it. Instead of bird watching, fish watching is the favorite pastime here. But I'm sure the sea monsters have scared away or eaten most of the sea life around the city."

Dr. Sykes stopped beside a silver pole as high as his head. He opened a little door, scanned his palm over a screen, and waited.

"Whom do you wish to call?" a man's voice asked.

"Admiral Jefferson! This is a Level 5 emergency," Dr. Sykes said.

While they waited, Luis walked across the road to a park. He sat on a bench and looked up at the bubble over the city.

"It's amazingly beautiful here this far underwater," Casey said. She sat down beside him and bent to touch the purple grass. Steel rolled across the ground and bumped into a tree. A large red nut dropped onto its head.

"It's probably fake," Luis said.

"No, it's all real," Casey said. "It feels different. Like, maybe some scientist cross-pollinated things and worked at growing stuff that could survive without any sun or wind or rain. They must pump freshwater up from below."

Luis watched the still flowers and trees. He hadn't noticed before that there wasn't any wind.

Dr. Sykes and Tyler walked across to them.

"We are to meet the admiral and his officers on board in half an hour," Dr. Sykes said. "You must be hungry. I will take you to my favorite restaurant. Then we board ship and set out for the underwater cave."

Luis suddenly heard his stomach growl. He didn't know what they ate in an under-the-sea city in the future, but he was hungry enough to try anything.

They walked two blocks past the tall buildings to smaller shops. Each was brightly painted as if to match the colorful fish that normally swam around the bubble city.

They followed the doctor into a blue building.

Luis picked up Steel and whispered, "I wish you could smell this, Uncle Cyrus. The food smells great."

"I haven't smelled food in a long, long time," Uncle Cyrus said. "Tesla's Time Twister keeps me alive somehow in the machine. But I very much miss the smell and taste of food."

Dr. Sykes ordered for all of them. They found a round table covered in a green cloth that looked like woven seaweed.

Within minutes, a woman brought out four plates and set them on the table.

"Wow, what's this?" Tyler asked. He poked a fork into a pile of orange goo.

"Try it," Dr. Sykes said. "I suppose you have never tasted anything like it in your time. Which is when, by the way?"

Luis bent down and sniffed the bright orange food. "We're from 2017."

"Ah," Dr. Sykes said. "Practically the dark times of knowledge."

"Hey," Casey said. "We're pretty smart and have created lots of new stuff. Our fathers are scientists. They are informed about the world."

"No offense, young lady," Dr. Sykes said.

Tyler slid his fork into the food on his plate and shoved it in his mouth. Luis waited to see if he would gag, choke, or spit out his food. Instead, Tyler grinned.

"This is great!" he said, taking another bite.

Dr. Sykes said, "It's a plant we found growing not far from where New Atlantis was built. It's full of vitamins and minerals and surprisingly full of flavor. There is lots of other natural food from the ocean here, but this is a favorite."

"I'd love to see this under a microscope," Tyler said.

Casey reached into her jacket and pulled a small bottle from a zippered pocket. She pulled out the stopper and gave it to her brother.

"Hey, thanks!" Tyler said. He scooped a little bit of the gooey, orange food into the bottle, closed it, and stuck it in his pocket.

They finished their meals in silence. Luis enjoyed the food, but he couldn't wait to get back on the *Neptune* and go to the cave Dr. Sykes had found. What was waiting for them that caused Dr. Sykes to not be surprised that they were from the past? And how could they get the sea monsters to leave before New Atlantis was destroyed?

Everything they needed to know to solve both problems and go home seemed to be in the cave.

And best of all, it would be a new adventure.

Then from above, Luis heard a loud crack. Outside, people screamed. A ceiling light in the restaurant dropped to the floor at Luis's feet.

Luis jumped up and ran outside. Tyler and Casey followed him. They looked up and saw one of the sea monsters ramming the top of the dome over and over. People were pointing and screaming.

"Quickly. To the submarine!" Dr. Sykes yelled. "Time is running out for the city."

Dr. Sykes ran down the street toward the docked submarine. Luis and his friends followed him. Luis held tightly onto Steel.

"I hope this man knows what he's doing," Uncle Cyrus said.

Luis agreed. The ground shook as the sea monsters rammed the dome again.

To the Cave!

Luis and his friends followed Dr. Sykes through the large hatch and into the submarine.

Several crew members were already inside, listening to a man explaining that they would need a crew of volunteers for the journey to the cave.

Everyone raised their hands.

Luis said, "They are all so brave."

Dr. Sykes said, "Yes, but they are also afraid. They all have family or friends in New Atlantis and want to know they are safe."

He hurried down the passageway that led to the control room.

The admiral turned and gasped. "Sykes! It's true! You really are awake!" He walked across the room and shook Dr. Sykes's hand. "We were all very worried about you."

Dr. Sykes sat down in a chair beside a tall machine covered in lights and strange symbols.

"I guess my mind couldn't handle what happened. I remember the cave. I remember exploring with my crew and studying the habits of the sea monsters we found on our first trip. But I don't remember getting back to the sub or returning home. And I don't remember what happened to my crew."

Luis felt bad for Dr. Sykes. He would be upset too if his friends suddenly disappeared.

Several men and women walked into the room and saluted the admiral.

"The crew is ready. Everyone wanted to come, so we drew lots for who would stay behind," a woman said.

"I'm not surprised." Admiral Jefferson nodded. "Then it's time to get moving. We'll have to get through those creatures surrounding the dome and speed to the cave as fast as the engines will allow."

Everyone began moving around the room, turning on the 3-D maps and navigation systems and sonar. Beeps echoed around the control room.

Luis looked at three dots on a radar screen that floated in the air. They moved around the city's dome. A red dot that wasn't moving was on a corner of the screen.

"That's us," the admiral explained. "We've got to slip out of here when the monsters are on the other side of the dome."

Casey unzipped one of her pockets and pulled out a small camera. She took a quick picture of the screen.

Tyler said, "I don't think it's a good idea to take a picture of future technology back to our time, Sis."

Casey said, "It's just for me. I promise. It'll go in my Journal of New Discoveries."

Luis said, "I never heard you talk about that before."

Casey whispered, "I never had one before. Not until we started traveling through time."

Steel rolled around the room, bumping into feet and machines.

"Beware of taking anything into another time other than what Tesla leaves for us," Uncle Cyrus said.

"Shh," Luis said. He looked across the room where the admiral and several crew were talking. "I don't want to have to explain all of this to everyone here."

Dr. Sykes clapped his hands. He bent down and picked up Steel off the floor.

"Is your cat-bot a time traveler also?"

Luis nodded. "He's actually the first time traveler. I mean, not the cat. The voice of the man trapped in Tesla's Time Twister comes through our robot cat."

He quickly told Dr. Sykes about his uncle, Tesla, Tesla's Time Twister, and the adventures they had gone on.

"Incredible!" Dr. Sykes said. "I would love to go with you on such an adventure."

"No, we have meddled enough in time and endangered ourselves," Uncle Cyrus said. Steam came out of Steel's ears.

The submarine slipped out of the docking station. Luis watched as the red dot moved. He could see the three black dots moving on the other side of the dome. He grabbed Tyler's arm as the *Neptune* moved faster.

"I'm okay. I won't fall," Tyler said.

"I'm not worried about that," Luis said. He pointed to the sonar screen. "I'm worried more about those black dots getting closer and the creatures noticing that we are leaving."

Casey ran to one of the windows that looked out into the ocean.

"I don't see anything coming," she said.

Admiral Jefferson said, "So far, they are still hovering around the opposite side of New Atlantis."

Dr. Sykes frowned. "That is good for us, but perhaps it is bad for the city. They may be preparing a large-scale attack."

"We've got to get to that cave fast!" Luis shouted.

The admiral responded, "Full speed!"

Luis could feel a shift in the submarine. Soon they were rushing past schools of fish.

Luis took Steel to a spot in the passageways away from everyone else.

"Uncle Cyrus, I don't know if we can take Steel with us to the cave. He's not really waterproof," Luis said.

Steel's red eyes blinked.

"You need to find a way to have the cat left near a communications system where I can hear and respond to what you are seeing. I need to know what Tesla left for me," Cyrus said.

Luis said, "I still don't understand why he left something here in the future."

"He didn't," Uncle Cyrus said. "I've done some research in the submarine's historical records through the Time Twister's connection to this ship. It seems that we are where New York and the upper East Coast once was, before a great earthquake that devastated the area. It's possible that this cave was once above ground."

"Oh! We learned about that earlier. There was a big earthquake in 2055," Luis said.

"Tesla may have left the message long ago, expecting me to find it, but not knowing it would be underwater," Uncle Cyrus said.

Casey and Tyler came out of the control room and sat down near Luis.

"This is amazing," Tyler said. "I've always dreamed of being an astronaut, but this is like being an *undersea* astronaut."

The submarine dipped as if they were going down deeper. Luis hurried back to the control room.

"What's going on?" he asked.

Admiral Jefferson said, "According to Dr. Sykes, we're nearing the cave. You three, the doctor, and two of my crew will take the minisub to the cave. We'll have the communications system open at all times."

Luis swallowed hard. They were about to get into a small underwater vessel and go into a cave known to have giant sea monsters.

"Sir, I need to have our robot cat able to hear us and communicate with me," Luis said.

The admiral raised his eyebrows. "Is this necessary?"

"Absolutely necessary," Tyler responded.

"Yes," Dr. Sykes said. "Please do as they say. We will go to the minisub and wait for your orders to depart."

Luis gave Steel to the admiral. "It's very important that nothing happens to this cat."

The admiral nodded.

Luis and his friends followed Dr. Sykes down a maze of passageways to a tall hatch.

Two crewmen were waiting. Name tags on their suits said Brody and Stephen. They opened the hatch and waited as Dr. Sykes, Luis, Tyler, and Casey went inside. The men followed them in and closed the hatch behind them.

Luis stared at the minisub. It wasn't much bigger than his bedroom.

"Six of us are going inside that?" Tyler asked.

Dr. Sykes said, "Yes, we'll be fine. There are underwater suits hanging on the wall. Quickly put them on and we'll board the minisub."

Luis pulled on a bright yellow suit. It felt

tight against his skin, but not uncomfortable. It had a helmet with tubes that attached to the suit.

"The commands are inside the helmet. Look at the icon and blink if you want to speak, need to use the boosters to move faster in the water, and so on."

"Wow," Tyler said. "Can I use this thing without my crutches?"

Dr. Sykes smiled. "Yes, I believe you'll find it quite amazing. Two of my crew had mobility issues and loved being in the water with this suit. You'll need help until we get into the water, but once outside the sub, you'll move as easily as the rest of us."

Everyone put on their suits in silence. Casey helped her brother.

"Are you ready, Dr. Sykes? We're near the cave. There is no sign of any giant sea monsters. You should go now."

"We're ready," Dr. Sykes said. He nodded at the others. "Let's get inside."

He turned to Luis as he opened the door to the minisub. "I have to admit that I am a little frightened. My last trip to the cave, I was the only one to return."

Luis wished Dr. Sykes had not reminded them that his last crew disappeared.

Luis took a deep breath and stepped into the minisub. There was no other way to find a way home.

Tesla's Message

Luis bumped his head on a corner of the minisub. "Ouch!"

"You'll get used to it," Dr. Sykes said. "We won't be in here long before we're out in the ocean."

There were seats along the sides of the minisub. Everyone sat down and Dr. Sykes flipped several switches. A 3-D screen came on and hovered in front of him.

He pointed to a dark spot on the screen.

"That is our cave. Hard to believe this was all on land once," Dr. Sykes said.

He touched the screen and suddenly water filled the room around the minisub. Then they were dropping down and out of the *Neptune.*

Luis stared out the window beside his seat. It was darker than the water around New Atlantis. He didn't see brightly colored fish or seaweed.

Something moved outside his window. He leaned closer to the glass.

Two eyes appeared out of the murky water and pressed against the other side of the glass. A small mouth with razor-sharp teeth appeared next.

Luis yelled and jumped back.

Dr. Sykes laughed. "You'll see worse than that. Don't lose your nerve now."

Tyler leaned across the aisle. "I hope Steel is okay and that your uncle doesn't say anything weird."

Luis didn't want to think what would happen to them if someone took apart Steel and they couldn't talk to Uncle Cyrus any longer.

The minisub slowed to a stop. Dr. Sykes gave each of them underwater flashlights. The two

ZOOM...
Zooooooм...

quiet crewmen checked everyone's oxygen levels on their suits.

"We'll be going about fifty yards from the sub," Dr. Sykes said.

"Brody and Stephen's job will be to watch for the sea monsters. They will warn us if they see one. I will show you the carved words in the cave wall. Then, we will explore the cave to see if anything might be displacing the creatures from their home."

They followed Dr. Sykes to the back of the sub. Stephen closed the steel door behind them. It sealed with a loud clank.

Casey grabbed her brother's arm as the room filled with water and Brody opened a hatch on the floor.

The crewmen jumped through the hatch door and into the ocean. Luis watched as Dr. Sykes followed them.

"Here we go," he said.

"Me first," Tyler said. He stepped forward, then grinned at Luis. "This walking stuff is pretty easy. Maybe I'll live underwater when we get home."

He jumped in and Casey followed him.

Luis took a step forward. One jump and he was in the ocean. He didn't want to think about the fish with the big eyes and bigger teeth.

He followed the others toward the mouth of the huge cave in front of the minisub. He thought about the cave in Star Wars that Han Solo's ship goes into, where it turns out to be the mouth of a giant creature.

"When we get inside, we'll go about 100 feet until we get to the tunnel where I found the writing. It's too small for the creatures, so we will be safe from them while you study it."

They passed through the mouth of the cave. Luis heard Casey gasp as bright colorful lights shone just inside the entrance.

"These are phosphorescent plants that grow along the walls," Dr. Sykes said. "I would like to take some samples back with us to study."

He swam to the cave wall and pulled a small pickax from a satchel around his neck. He broke away the rock around a few of the plants and stuffed them inside the satchel. Red, green, and blue lights shone through the bag.

Luis, Tyler, and Casey followed him through the enormous cave. Outside the entrance, the two crewmen watched for any of the creatures to come inside. Luis was more worried about the ones that were already inside.

Bubbles suddenly surrounded them. The dark water shook like a watery earthquake as a giant sea creature rose up beside them.

"I knew it!" Luis yelled.

Luis stared at the whale-like creature. Instead of a blowhole on its head, long octopus tentacles waved in the water, reaching out toward them.

"Quickly, follow me," Dr. Sykes said. "We are near the tunnel."

The sea monster's huge eyes followed them as they swam toward a small tunnel a few feet away.

Dr. Sykes slipped inside, then reached a hand out to pull Tyler and Casey in behind him.

Luis was last. When he grabbed at Dr. Sykes's hand, he felt a tug on his foot.

Luis looked back and saw one of the tentacles had wrapped around his foot and was pulling him toward the sea monster's mouth.

Tyler shot out of the tunnel. He grabbed both of Luis's hands with his and began pulling.

Luis felt like a rope in tug-of-war. He tried kicking the tentacle off with his other foot.

Something rushed past him. Then suddenly, the tentacle let go and his foot was free.

"Go! Quick!" Casey shouted as she swam beside Luis and Tyler.

They swam for the tunnel. Luis felt pressure behind them. Something big was moving through the water. He did not want to look back.

Dr. Sykes pulled them into the cavern. They backed away even more as a tentacle slid in after them. But after several moments, it pulled away.

"Wow, that was close!" Tyler said.

Luis's heart pounded like a drum. He gave Tyler a hug. "Thanks for coming after me."

Tyler said, "I've never moved so fast, even when I spent some time in an electric wheelchair. It was great!"

"And what about me?" Casey said.

Luis grinned. "Did you get that monster's tentacle off my foot?"

She nodded. "I may not have my coat, but I have to carry something with me or I feel weird."

Casey pulled a folding knife from a pocket in her scuba suit. "It even has a bottle opener in case we get thirsty for a soda."

Dr. Sykes folded his arms, floating backward in the water. "You three gave me quite a scare. I've not seen such bravery since my crew . . ."

He looked away. "I wish I knew what happened to them. Five of the bravest men and women you'd ever meet." He turned away and said, "Follow me."

Luis glanced back at the entrance to the tunnel. He could see one huge eye staring back at him. The creature was waiting for them to come out.

"Over here," Dr. Sykes said.

Luis looked at an icon on the screen in his helmet. It looked like the *Neptune.* He hoped it was the right one to communicate with the submarine.

"Uncle Cyrus? Are you there?" Luis asked.

There was nothing but static.

"Uncle Cyrus? We're at the cave. We're about to see the message," Luis said.

"I'm here, Luis," Uncle Cyrus said. "Is everyone safe?"

Luis said, "Yes. One of the sea monsters came after us. But we're okay for now. I'll tell you when we see the message."

He followed the others through the tunnel. It was a tight squeeze, but after a moment the tunnel opened wide.

Dr. Sykes pointed to one side of the tunnel. The glowing plants were better than flashlights.

"Do you see it?" Uncle Cyrus asked.

Luis moved closer to the wall. There were words carved into it. Some of the plants had grown over them.

"Yeah, I can see it," Luis said. "It looks like Tesla used some kind of heavy tool and scratched the words into the tunnel wall."

"Hurry! Read them to me!" Cyrus shouted.

Luis ran his hands over the wall and tried to push the plants aside.

"Help me," he said.

Casey and Tyler pulled at the plants.

"Don't waste them," Dr. Sykes said, holding out his bag.

When the plants had been cleared around the carved words, Luis moved his fingers across the letters.

"I can read it now," he said.

"Then do so," Cyrus ordered.

Luis read the words to himself and frowned. He took a deep breath and read aloud, "Time is not our friend. There is great danger in changing it." He didn't want to read on.

"Is that all, Luis." Uncle Cyrus sounded as if he were struggling not to cry.

Luis looked at his friends. He read the rest. "Do not return home, Cyrus. Your friend through all time, Nikola Tesla."

MONSTER EGGS

Luis heard Cyrus gasp. He swallowed hard.

"What does it mean?" Casey asked.

Cyrus spoke softly. "It means that I cannot return home to my time. Tesla has rightly realized that my reality has changed. If I go back, I change and influence the people and events I would become a part of and risk changing the future that comes after the day I return."

Luis said, "So this has all been for nothing? You're trapped in time forever?"

Dr. Sykes touched Luis's shoulder.

"You have a lot to talk about with your friend. For now, we must leave this tunnel and try to discover what has caused the sea creatures to attack New Atlantis," said Dr. Sykes.

"We'll be stuck in time too if we don't finish this," Tyler said. "Although, if it weren't for my family and friends back in my time, I'd stay here and walk in the ocean every day."

Dr. Sykes pointed down the tunnel. "We have no other choice but to go back the way we came. I'll go first. I do not know why Stephen and Brody didn't warn us about the creature that attacked earlier, but we need to go deeper into the cave."

He swam past them and back to the beginning of the tunnel. Dr. Sykes waved for them to stay behind him as he looked out the entrance.

He returned, saying, "I don't see any of the giant creatures. We should move quickly. They have a known lair close to this tunnel."

Luis helped Casey and Tyler go through the small entrance. Then he squeezed out. He waited for a tentacle to grab him again, but nothing came.

They followed Dr. Sykes farther into the cave. Luis thought they must all be crazy to get closer to the giant sea monsters' lair.

"Wow, look at the glowing plants," Tyler said. "They're getting thicker the deeper we go."

Dr. Sykes said, "Yes, it appears that the sea monsters and the plants live well together. Perhaps the creatures fertilize the plants."

A loud roar surrounded them. Luis held his hands against his helmet. "Ouch, I didn't think fish made noises underwater."

Dr. Sykes said, "Deep in these waters, there are many unusual sea creatures. You have seen how strange they look. The fact that they growl like roaring lions is strange, but not surprising."

Another roar shook the cave.

"I will go ahead," Dr. Sykes said. "You three stay here where it's safe."

"Safe?" Casey asked. "There's nowhere safe in this cave. We're coming too."

They followed Dr. Sykes and were soon in a wide opening in the underwater cave.

Luis waited for one of the sea monsters to come after them. But the roaring had stopped.

"Hey, look at this!" Casey yelled.

She sat on a stone ledge that stuck out from the cave wall. Luis swam closer and saw dozens of large, round, white balls.

"What are those?" Luis asked. "They look like bowling balls glued together."

Dr. Sykes hurried to the ledge. He floated around the white balls. "Amazing. You have found a batch of eggs!"

Casey's eyes widened. "Sea monster eggs? Wow. Well that's both exciting and scary."

Luis touched one of the eggs. It felt slimy and wiggled at his touch.

Dr. Sykes said, "My men who came back to this part of the cave did not tell me of these eggs. These are close to hatching."

Luis could see strange shadows inside. A red eye peered at him from one of the eggs.

"I don't think we'd better be here when one of those sea monsters comes back," Casey said. "You know how protective moms are of their babies."

Dr. Sykes shouted, "That's it!"

He swam around the group of eggs and looked at them. Luis watched him peeking all around the group of eggs and under the shelf.

Dr. Sykes motioned for them to come closer. "Look, in that corner under the shelf. Do you see? There is a big hole right in the middle of the clutch of eggs. There are several that are missing."

Luis shrugged. "Maybe they just fell off and floated away."

Dr. Sykes said, "No, look closely. You will see marks from tools. Someone pried them away."

Tyler said, "Who would do that? Why?"

"Some of my crew must have done it. They probably just wanted to study them, but they should have known better," Dr. Sykes said.

Luis now understood why the sea monsters were attacking New Atlantis.

"The eggs are back in the city, aren't they?" Luis said.

The doctor nodded. "My sub was taken back to the city when I was discovered alone inside. I feel sure the eggs are somewhere on board. And the sea monsters will do anything to get them back."

A voice came through the speaker in their helmets.

"This is Admiral Jefferson. The crewmen saw several creatures heading your way. They went back to the minisub and are on their way to rescue you. Get out of that cave!"

Dr. Sykes said, "Good. We need to get back to the *Neptune* right away. Admiral, get ready to hurry back to New Atlantis. We know how to stop the monsters. That is, if we're not too late."

Luis turned when Casey screamed.

A giant snake of a sea monster with slit eyes and wing-like fins came straight at them.

Dr. Sykes shouted, "Hold hands and swim!"

They grabbed one another's hands and swam away from the eggs. Luis saw the sea monster stop beside the eggs and nose them as if counting.

"There's the minisub!" Tyler yelled.

The little submarine sped toward them. As soon as it stopped, Dr. Sykes led them to the hatch. They swam through the hatch. Inside, Stephen tightened the hatch cover and drained the seawater from the room.

"We have to get back to the *Neptune* as fast as possible," Dr. Sykes said.

They found their seats and watched as the two men touched points on the 3-D screen. The minisub turned and sped through the water.

"Uh, I think we're in trouble," Tyler said.

Luis looked out his window and saw two sea monsters following them. One looked like a giant largemouth bass. Its mouth opened as if to swallow them.

"Hurry!" Luis shouted. "They're getting closer!"

He could see the *Neptune* ahead of them. They were close. Close enough to see that two more sea monsters had surrounded the submarine.

"How will we get inside the *Neptune*?" Tyler asked.

Dr. Sykes pressed his face against a window. "I don't know if we can get inside."

Luis watched as one of the sea monsters came closer. It opened its mouth wider.

The lights in the minisub went out as the sea monster swallowed them.

Baby Monsters

Luis could see nothing in the darkness.

There was lots of noise. The sound of Brody and Stephen yelling at the minisub's computer to turn on again. The sound of Dr. Sykes banging on the roof of the minisub to scare the monster. And the sound of the monster's growls deep in its throat.

After several moments, the lights flickered back on in the minisub and the computer's 3-D screens returned.

It didn't make anyone feel much better. Now Luis could see pink sliminess all around them.

"We're in the creature's mouth!" Tyler yelled.

"That's good," Dr. Sykes said. "We haven't been swallowed yet."

Casey said, "We need to find a way to make him spit us out." She jumped up and moved around the minisub.

She looked behind the seats and at the back of the sub. "Doesn't this thing have any weapons?"

Dr. Sykes shook his head. "This is an exploratory sub. It is for research only."

Casey said, "I don't want to kill it, but we need to scare it a little."

Brody said, "We have a laser to cut through rock and thick seaweed."

"Perfect," Casey said. "Where is it?"

Brody pointed to a symbol on the 3-D screen. "That turns on the beam and those arrows will aim it wherever you want."

Casey smiled. "Does that mean I get to use it?" She looked beyond thrilled.

"Yes!" Luis shouted. "Just get us out of here!"

Casey pressed the symbol on the screen for the laser. A red stream shot from the minisub.

The sea monster roared and began to roll.

"Hey, we need him to open his mouth," Tyler said as he grabbed onto his chair, "not spin like a top."

Casey pressed the arrows up and down until the beam shot toward the mouth of the monster. It roared again and opened its mouth. The minisub was quickly flung back into the ocean.

"Ooh, I think it vomited us out," Luis said.

Casey shot the beam of light toward the creatures surrounding the *Neptune*. They bellowed at the laser, then shot past the minisub and away from the large submarine.

"You did it!" Luis said.

Casey grinned.

Dr. Sykes pointed toward the *Neptune*. "Get us there before they come back."

Before he could say "sea monster!" Luis was off the minisub, out of his underwater suit, and running with the others to the command area.

"We're on our way back home," Admiral Jefferson said. "What happened in the cave?"

Dr. Sykes explained about the eggs as they sped back to New Atlantis.

They waited again for the sea monsters that circled the city to be on the other side of the dome before the *Neptune* slipped into the dock.

They left the submarine as Admiral Jefferson led Dr. Sykes, Luis and his friends, and Steel through the streets.

"I know where your submarine is," the admiral told Dr. Sykes. "It hasn't been touched since

they brought you here. It's been in quarantine since it was checked over after you went into your coma." He stopped at a parking garage and spoke with a woman who gave him five keys.

Admiral Jefferson handed out the keys. "It will take too long to walk. So, we ride," he said.

They followed him into the parking garage and pointed to five of the chair-cars.

"Wow, we get to use these?" Luis asked.

Casey said, "But, we're not old enough to have driver's licenses."

Dr. Sykes laughed. "Anyone ten and above can drive the transports. They run by voice command."

Luis helped Tyler into one of the chairs and then found his own. He felt like he was about to ride some strange kind of bumper car. There were no wheels or doors.

Luis put the key into a spot in front of him. A 3-D screen appeared.

"We're going to the Science Center," the admiral said. "Just tell it that location and it will take you there."

"Science Center," Luis said. He heard the others speak to their chairs.

Suddenly he was zipping through the streets, floating over the road. The chairs passed other people in chair-cars. Some people were reading, watching a movie, or eating a meal. But everyone was keeping an eye on the dome.

"Hey, can you build something like this, Tyler?" Luis yelled.

Tyler shouted back, "I wish. Even if I could, how would it work on our streets?"

The chairs turned off the main road and into the parking garage of a round building.

Admiral Jefferson led them into the building and to an elevator. He waved at a guard, who nodded.

"Sublevel 3," he said to the elevator.

Luis felt them moving down. The doors opened to a large warehouse. In one corner, a submarine sat on the floor. It had scratches and bite marks on its sides.

Dr. Sykes ran to the sub and rubbed his hands over one of the scratches. "We must've been attacked by the monsters. I do not know how we . . . I escaped them."

Luis climbed a ladder to the top level of the sub. "Where do you think the eggs might be?"

Dr. Sykes said, "I have a secret water-filled compartment that I use to bring specimens home. Go inside the submarine and look under the last seat on the left. There will be a lever to move the seat forward, and a voice command beneath. Say my name and it will open. Parker Sykes."

Luis opened a small hatch and climbed down into the submarine. It was bigger than the minisub, but much smaller than the *Neptune*.

He ran down the hall to the front of the submarine. Four chairs were against each side of the sub. He stopped at the back one on the left and felt for a lever.

"Got it!" he said.

The chair moved forward. Beneath it was a blinking red light.

Luis bent down and said, "Parker Sykes."

He jumped back when a square metal container rose from the floor. It stopped when it was as tall as his waist. A slit appeared in the top and folded open.

Luis looked into the container. It was filled with water. He reached inside and felt something round and slimy. There were several of the slimy objects.

The sea monster eggs!

Luis ran back to the hatch that led up to the top of the submarine.

"They're here. The eggs are here!" he shouted.

Casey clapped her hands.

Admiral Jefferson wiped his brow with a handkerchief. "Good job, everyone."

Dr. Sykes climbed up to where Luis stood. "Now we've got them. All we have to do is give them back to the sea monsters so they will leave New Atlantis alone."

Luis groaned. "And how are we going to do that?"

Dr. Sykes put a hand on Luis's shoulder. "We will have to take the eggs outside ourselves so the sea monsters can see them."

Luis looked down at his friends. "Sure, nothing to it," he said. "All we have to do is make sure they don't eat us before they see the eggs."

HOME, FOR EVERYONE

Luis stood in a glass elevator with Dr. Sykes, Tyler, and Casey. He tugged at his face mask and tapped his oxygen tank. Unlike Tyler, he wasn't thrilled about getting back into the suit.

The elevator dropped below the streets of New Atlantis and into a small room that filled with seawater.

Then, the elevator door opened from the bottom and they floated out into the ocean.

Luis grabbed the net bag full of the strange sea monster eggs. They were beginning to glow. He could see lots of eyes staring through the eggs.

"What if the creatures don't find us?" Casey asked.

"I don't think that'll be a problem," Tyler said. He pointed ahead of them. One of the giant monsters hurtled through the water.

"It's coming straight at us!" Luis yelled.

The sea monster had bulging stalk eyes and feather-looking flippers. Like the others, its mouth was filled with huge, pointed teeth.

Dr. Sykes said, "Just stay still and don't move. Luis, get ready to release those eggs. Hold them up first so the creature can see them."

Luis held the eggs high over his head.

The eggs glowed brighter.

The sea monster stopped suddenly, as if slamming on the brakes. Then another sea monster came toward them and circled their group.

"We're surrounded," Casey whispered.

"Stay calm," Dr. Sykes said. "They want the eggs, not us."

Luis hoped he was right.

The first sea monster moved closer and nudged the bag of eggs.

Luis didn't know what to do. "Should I just let the eggs out of the net or let go of the net and have the sea monster move it back to the cave somehow?"

Before Dr. Sykes could answer, an egg popped. A sea monster the size of Luis's head sat in the net staring at him. Its little jaws opened to show small sharp teeth.

Then another egg popped, and then another.

"Wow," Casey said. "For sea monsters, they're kind of cute."

Luis held the net away from him. "Yeah, cute with lots of teeth."

When the last egg popped, the adult sea monsters roared. Luis shook the net until it opened and the babies swam out. They looked at Luis a moment, then turned and swam toward the adults.

With a final roar, the giant sea monsters and babies swam away.

"We did it!" Tyler yelled.

Luis grinned as he felt the tug of Tesla's Time Twister. He watched the water swirl around him and his friends. Dr. Sykes's eyes were wide. Luis waved at him until he went into the white cloud of time. He closed his eyes and remembered that Steel was still on the *Neptune.*

When he opened his eyes, they were back in the Time Twister. Steel sat on his lap.

MEOW! MEOW! MEOW!

Tyler jumped up. "Hey, did you hear? It sounds like a regular cat."

Uncle Cyrus's voice said, "They took the cat to Bot Repair while you were saving New Atlantis."

Tyler said, "That's great. But I sure wish I could've seen it."

Casey stood and stretched. "I'm glad to be

back home. I couldn't really use my gadgets underwater."

Luis put Steel on the floor. "But what about you, Uncle Cyrus? We went there to help you, but Tesla told you not to try to go back to your time."

Uncle Cyrus said, "I must agree with my friend. My desire to get out of this machine's pull and back home has clouded my thoughts. It is not safe to change my time line now."

Casey patted Steel's back. "But it's not fair for you to be stuck in here forever."

Luis snapped his fingers. He pulled the melded pocket watch and gold scarab from his pocket.

"This grounded you to our time, right?" Luis said.

He held it out and waved it around the time machine. Uncle Cyrus's body began to take shape.

After a moment, he faded away again.

Luis groaned. "It's not working. I think we needed something from our last trip in time."

This time, Tyler snapped his fingers. He reached into his back pocket and pulled out the small container Casey had given him. Inside, the orange food from their meal in the future sparkled. "Try this," he said.

Luis opened the bottle and poured the food from New Atlantis onto the watch and scarab. The orange food turned hard, like glue. Luis squeezed the melded ball in his hand. He held it out.

Uncle Cyrus's shimmering body returned.

Luis dropped the watch and scarab into his great-great-great-great-uncle's hand. When it landed, Cyrus stood in front of them, just as solid as they were.

"I am solid. I am myself again!" Cyrus said.

"Stay with us, Uncle Cyrus," Luis said.

"Are you certain?" Cyrus asked.

Luis said, "You can live here and work with our dads. You helped build this machine. You know all about it. And you've seen time go by. We could have more great adventures together."

Uncle Cyrus squeezed the object in his hand. "It's not home, but being with you all is beginning to feel like home."

Luis reached out and touched his uncle's arm. Tyler opened the door of Tesla's Time Twister. Casey carried Steel into the shed. Tyler stepped out and Luis followed, arm in arm with his uncle.

His father and Mr. Jenson stood in front of the Time Twister.

"Dad!" Luis yelled.

His father ran up the steps. "I thought I'd lost you," he said. He frowned at Luis. "I don't know whether to be the happiest man on earth, or ground you until your hair turns gray."

He pulled Luis into a hug. Casey and Tyler hurried to their dad and began telling him of their adventures.

Luis's dad pulled away and stared at Uncle Cyrus.

"Who's this?" he asked.

Luis said, "Dad, meet your great-great-great-uncle Cyrus. He built the Time Twister with Tesla. He's the one who wrote the journal."

Mr. Sanchez pulled Luis toward him. "Impossible. Cyrus is long dead."

Uncle Cyrus put the watch-scarab into his pocket. He held out his hand to Mr. Sanchez.

"I'm truly happy to meet you, nephew. I am not dead. I have simply been trapped in time all these years. Your son and his friends have rescued me."

Luis's father's mouth dropped open.

Luis and his friends explained everything that had happened in the last few days. When they were done, the room was quiet except for Steel's meows.

"Amazing. Shocking. Unbelievable," Mr. Jenson said.

"Dad, can Uncle Cyrus stay with us? He's alone in this time. He can help you two a lot," Luis said.

His father looked from Luis to the Time Twister. "It really works?" He shook hands with Uncle Cyrus. "Welcome to our home. And our time."

Then Mr. Sanchez frowned at Luis and his friends. "We will be having a long talk about the danger you have put yourself in without us knowing about it."

Luis swallowed hard. "Okay, Dad."

Uncle Cyrus said, "I'm sorry. Much of that has been my fault. I know that I will have many things to learn here. And, many things to show you about Tesla's machine."

Luis nudged his dad. "Maybe we can all take a trip together next time."

His father glanced at Mr. Jenson. "We will have to discuss that a great deal."

Mr. Sanchez and Mr. Jenson walked with Uncle Cyrus out of the shed. The three men talked as if they were old friends. Luis and his friends followed.

"Looks like we've got a new relative living with us," Luis said.

Casey and Tyler nodded.

"Do you think our fathers will let us Time Twist again?" Casey asked.

Luis glanced back at the shed. He knew his father would want to test the machine. And when he did, Luis was going to make sure they shared the adventure.

"I guess we'll have to wait and see," Luis said. "Tesla was wrong. Time is on our side. We just have to use it carefully."

Luis raced his friends to the back porch. Spring break had been full of adventure. School was starting soon, but he wasn't worried about being bored.

He looked back at the shed. Tesla's Time Twister would be waiting for other adventures in other times.

2018